Bicycle Riding

and Other Poems

by Sandra Olson Liatsos
Illustrated by Karen Dugan

Wordsong/Boyds Mills Press

To my husband for his loyalty,
to my parents for all of their wonderful gifts,
and to all, everywhere.

— S.O.L.

For Mrs. Marcia Dugan, with love, Karen

—K.D.

ACKNOWLEDGMENTS

Some of the poems in this book first appeared with the following publishers:

Macmillan/McGraw Hill, *Stepping Stones*, "Bicycle Riding," "Leaf Birds."

Open Court Publishing, *Cricket Magazine*, "Bicycle Riding," "Fishermen's Beach."

National Wildlife Federation, Ranger Rick magazine, "Sea Wave," "Climbing Trees," "Waterfall,"
"Seashell," "Leaf Birds," "Camping in My Yard."

World Book Incorporated, *I Was Wondering, a Childcraft Book*, "Seashell."

Text copyright © 1997 by Sandra Olson Liatsos
Illustrations copyright © 1997 by Karen Dugan
All rights reserved

Published by Wordsong
Boyds Mills Press
815 Church Street
Honesdale, Pennsylvania 18431
Printed in Mexico

Publisher Cataloging-in-Publication Data
Liatsos, Sandra Olson.
Bicycle riding / by Sandra Olson Liatsos; illustrated by Karen Dugan—1st ed.
[32]p. : ill.; cm.
Summary: A collection of poems that explore a variety of warm weather activities and outings.
ISBN 1-56397-235-2
1. Children's Poetry, American. 2. Bicycles and bicycling—Juvenile poetry.
[1. American poetry. 2. Bicycles and bicycling —Poetry. Outdoor recreation—Poetry.]
I. Dugan, Karen, ill. II. Title.
811.54-dc20   1997   AC   CIP
Library of Congress Catalog Card Number 96-83924

First edition, 1997
Book designed by Tim Gillner
The text of this book was set in 14-point Goudy.
The illustrations are done in Watercolor.

10 9 8 7 6 5 4 3 2 1

CONTENTS

BICYCLE RIDING

My feet rise
off the planet,
pedal wheels of steel
that sparkle as
they spin me through
the open space I feel—
winging out
to galaxies
far beyond the sun,
where bicycles
are satellites,
their orbits never done.

THE HERO OF OUR STREET

When our tongues are oven-dry
 And steamy puddles fill our shoes,
When we drag from base to base
 In a game we're sure to lose,
Then the hero of our street
 Rescues us from summer heat.
Through the steamy, city sun
 His caravan is on the run.

"Lemon! Orange! Chocolate! Lime!
Give three cheers for ice-cream time!
With flavors frozen close to zero,
He's our favorite ice-cream hero!"

Gobbling cold we wipe our faces.
Then we whip around the bases!

SEA WAVE

It tumbled and it crumbled
Like a mountain in a quake.
It thundered and I wondered
At the power it could make.
It trickled and it tickled me.
I saw it disappear.
The mountain was a murmuring
Of ocean in my ear.

LISTENING TO A SEASHELL

When I hear the waves
Tumble in a shell,
I feel as though
I've stepped inside
To where sea creatures dwell.
I swim about their thunder-world
Of waves that roll and roar,
Then ride them on their secret sea
They let just me explore.

EATING BLUEBERRIES

We found them
    Big as marbles
And we rolled them
    In our mouths
And bit them
    Till the juice
Ran down in rivers.

We gathered
    And we feasted
Till our teeth
    Turned berry-blue
And now
    Our smiles
Give everyone
    The shivers.

CAMPING IN MY YARD

I'm trying to sleep
beneath the stars
the way the foxes do,
in my pup tent
    opened up
to sky
that once was blue.
The night
has spread its magic.
I can feel it in the air . . .

In dreams
I'll be
a daring fox
    leaping from my lair.

CLIMBING TREES

It isn't easy
climbing trees,
but that's what makes
it fun.
You need to win them
step by step.
You cannot trot
or run.
You need to sweat
and sweat some more
until you reach
the top.
But then you feel
as if you'll never
really have to stop,
as if your arms
will turn to wings
and you will learn
to fly
to trees
in other galaxies
that lead
to the farthest sky.

THE BAREBACK RIDER AT THE CIRCUS

His cape flew out in the rushing wind.
  The sparks lit up on his uniform.
He looked like a bolt of summer lightning
  Riding upon a thunderstorm.

WATERFALL

Top to bottom see it fall,
White and silver rushing,
As if the world had tipped too far
And spilled its river gushing
Over rims of rock and stone
To thunder in a pool,
To glow and bubble in the sun,
To hold and keep me cool.

AUGUST

August
  breathes
    hot
    tiger-breath
on my burning skin
and stalks me
    to the icy river
where I plunge right in.

August
  crouches
    on the bank
and steams
    in its own heat.
I'd like to drag it
    in with me
and freeze it
    ears to feet.

AT THE PARADE

The balloon man hobbles and wobbles along
In time to the marching, in time to the song.
Beneath his beguiling and bobbling tree
He calls, "Balloons! Buy balloons from me!"

We follow the bulbous yellows and greens,
The orange and purply peacock-sheens.
The clink of our pennies can never compare
To those beautiful balls that can float on the air.

We carry them proudly behind the parade
As if we had made them in summery shade,
As if we had given them magic to fly
And, then, they chose us instead of the sky.

WHO NEEDS A BANQUET?

Who needs a banquet
fit for kings?
Who needs a heap
of jeweled rings?
Who needs a million
dollar jet
or a diamond collar
for a pet?
When bubbly pizza
from the oven
makes me grab
my fork and knife,
I need no more—
except a plate,
to lead a happy
pizza life.

NIGHT MUSIC

In the night
I heard a loon
laughing low and long,
as though he knew
his silver laugh
was an evening song.

In the night
I hear a coyote
crooning at the moon,
as though he knew
his wildest voice
sang a nighttime tune.

In my bed
I heard myself
sing in starry light
with the loon and coyote,
a song about the night.

LEAFY SEA

Tide high on a leafy sea,
Run with me in waves of elm.
Mound up an ocean
In your hand,
Catch the water,
Each pointed crest.
Parade the sea
In the deep
Red, gold,
And plum-light leaves.

ON A WINDY DAY

    The scarecrow tips
His hat at me.
He waves a stringy hand.
He does a funny
Kick as if
He'll dance across the land.
    I laugh to see him
come alive.
I greet him with a grin
and tell him,
"Lucky that
your friend
is lively Mr. Wind."

LEAF BIRDS

Fly, leaves, fly
From your maple tree.
Dive, leaves, dive
Down to play with me.
Rise, leaves, rise
When I throw you high.
Fly like birds
Closer to the sky.

WILD GEESE

When I watch
Their flock in flight
And when I hear their cries
I wonder how
They always know
Their way through
Distant skies.

PUMPKIN PICKING

Let's go picking in the pumpkin patch.
Now we're jiggling the old gate latch.
Gate swings wide and we step inside.
Pumpkins spread like an ocean tide.
You take the one like a fat balloon.
I'll take the one like an orange moon.
Hike to the house in fifty paces.
Then we'll carve out the pumpkin faces.

WOLF CRY

The wolf cries at night.
I hear the mountains
on the moon
tremble.
Shivers
slide down my spine.
I float
above the moon's
craters where
the silver wolves
make their caves.

SEASHELL

This seashell is an ocean cove
That holds a liquid sound
Of waves that rush a hidden shore
Where stranger shells are found.
Shells that whisper secrets
Of how the ocean grew,
Shells that know which stories
Of the sea are really true.

FISHERMEN'S BEACH

We wondered how
the fishermen
could stand the wooden
lobster house
full of old traps
that reeked of dead fish.

We wanted to be gulls
soaring over waves,
swooping down to catch
fish to eat a picnic
high on the rocks
where sea-smells
and rock-smells
were part of the fish
going down slippery
inside of us
quick and clean
as sea wind.

BUTTERFLIES

Why do the butterflies
fly out to sea
    over the rocks
      where waves roar at me?

They must be as brave
as sea lions who sing
    to fly near high waves
      with their delicate wings.